Big Book of Just So Stories

Miles Kelly

First published in 2016 by Miles Kelly Publishing Ltd
Harding's Barn, Bardfield End Green, Thaxted, Essex, CM6 3PX, UK

Copyright © Miles Kelly Publishing Ltd 2016

This edition printed 2017

2 4 6 8 10 9 7 5 3

Publishing Director Belinda Gallagher
Creative Director Jo Cowan
Editorial Director Rosie Neave
Designers Jo Cowan, Simon Lee, Joe Jones, Rob Hale
Production Elizabeth Collins, Caroline Kelly
Reprographics Stephan Davis, Jennifer Cozens, Thom Allaway
Assets Lorraine King

ISBN 978-1-78617-016-3

Printed in China

British Library Cataloguing-in-Publication Data
A catalogue record for this book is available from the British Library

ACKNOWLEDGEMENTS
The publishers would like to thank the following artists who have contributed to this book:
How the Camel Got His Hump: Marta Álvarez
How the Leopard Got His Spots: Kimberley Scott
How the Rhinoceros Got His Skin: Illustrations copyright © 2016 Daron Parton
How the Whale Got His Throat: Claudia Ranucci

Made with paper from a sustainable forest

www.mileskelly.net

How the Camel got his Hump

In the beginning of years when the world was new, there was a camel.

The camel did not want to work for the man like the other animals, so he lived in the middle of the Howling Desert. He ate sticks and prickles, and was most idle.

4

When anybody spoke
to him he said,

"Humph!"

Just 'Humph!' and no more.

5

On Monday the horse went to see the camel. The horse had a saddle on his back and a bit in his mouth.

He said, "Camel, come out and trot like the rest of us."

6

"Humph!"

said the camel. And the horse went away and told the man.

7

On **Tuesday** the dog went to see the camel. The dog had a stick in his mouth.

He said, "Camel, come and fetch like the rest of us."

8

"Humph!"

said the camel. And
the dog went away and
told the man.

9

On **Wednesday** the ox went to see the camel. The ox had a yoke on his neck.

He said, "Camel, come and **plough** like the rest of us."

10

"HUMPH!"
said the camel. And the ox
went away and told the man.

11

That evening the man called the horse and the dog and the ox together.

He said, "That camel in the Howling Desert won't work. You three must work double to make up for it."

13

So the three animals went to the genie in charge of all deserts and told him their problem.

The horse said, "There's an animal in the middle of your Howling Desert who is idle, and won't work."

14

"That's my camel!" said the genie in surprise. "What does he say about it?"

"He says 'Humph!'" said the ox. The genie flew off at once.

15

The genie found the camel being idle. "Camel, what's this I hear of you doing no work?" asked the genie.

"Humph!" said the camel. So the genie began to think a great magic.

16

"You've given everyone extra work ever since Monday, all on account of your idleness," the genie went on.

"Humph!"

said the camel. So the genie went on thinking a great magic.

17

"I shouldn't say that again if I were you," said the genie. "You might say it once too often. Camel, I want you to **work**."

18

But the camel only said

"Humph!"

again.

No sooner had the camel said 'Humph!' a third time than his back began puffing up into a great big humph!

"There!" said the genie. "That's your very own humph that you've brought upon your very own self by not working."

20

"But how can I work with this humph on my back?" cried the camel.

"You would not work for three days. Your new humph lets you work for three days without eating," said the genie.

21

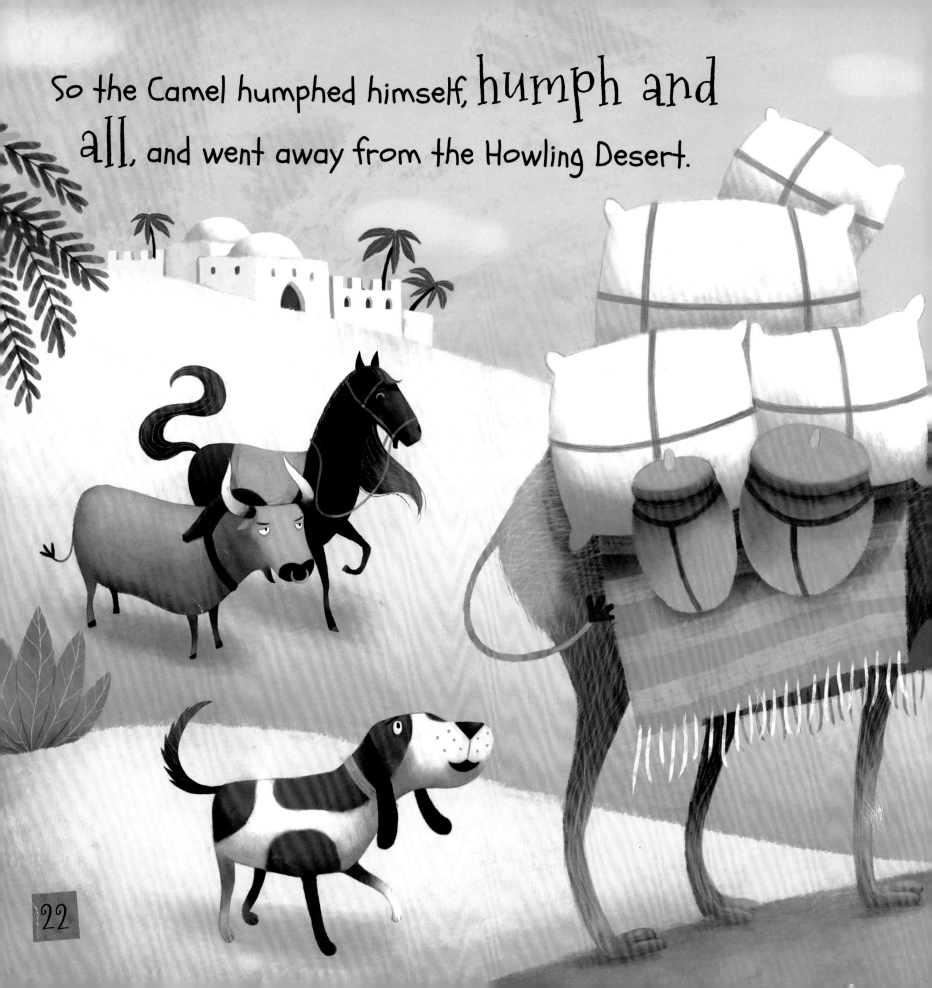

So the Camel humphed himself, humph and all, and went away from the Howling Desert.

And from that day to this, the camel always has a humph – but we call it a hump now, so as not to hurt his feelings.

But he has never yet caught up with the three days that he missed at the beginning of the world.

23

And he has never yet
learned how to behave.

24

How the Leopard got his Spots

There was once a **leopard** who had a yellowish-brownish coat. Everything around him...

the grass

the rocks

the animals

...was a yellowish-brownish colour too.

The leopard was hardest to spot, so it was
easy for him to sneak up on other animals
and eat them for dinner!

27

The leopard would hide behind a yellowish-brownish rock, or lie in the tall yellowish-brownish grass. Then he would leap out!

Yikes!

28

Sometimes the leopard hunted with his friend the man. Then the other animals didn't know which way to jump!

So bit by bit (the giraffe began it, because his legs were the longest) the animals scuttled off to find a place to hide.

At last they came to a great forest. The trees and bushes cast **stripy, speckly** shadows.

After a long time of standing with the **slippery, slidy** shadows falling on them, the giraffe grew blotchy and the zebra grew stripy and the antelope grew darker.

At last you could hear them and smell them, but you could **hardly see them at all.**

Meanwhile, the leopard and the man were looking all over their yellowish-brownish home, wondering where all their **breakfasts** and **lunches** and **dinners** had gone!

They were so hungry that they had to eat beetles and rats.

Then they both had **terrible** tummy-ache together.

Ouch!

So the leopard and the man went to see the baboon, who was quite the wisest animal they knew. The leopard asked, "Where has our breakfast gone?"

The baboon said to the man, "My friend, your breakfast decided it was time for a change. You should change, too."

Then the baboon winked, and said, "Leopard, your breakfast has gone into other spots. You should do the same."

So the leopard and the man set off to look for their breakfast. At last they came to a great forest, full of spotty, dotty shadows.

"What is this?" asked the leopard. "I can hear zebra, and I can smell zebra, but I can't see zebra."

"It's strange," agreed the man. "I can hear giraffe, and I can smell giraffe, but I can't see giraffe."

37

That night, the leopard heard something moving in the dark, so he jumped on top of it. It felt like zebra. It smelled like zebra.

CRASH!

He heard the man catch something too. They decided to sit on these strange, invisible things until morning.

In the morning they looked at what they had caught. The man said, "Mine looks like giraffe, but it is covered with brown blotches."

Leopard said, "Mine looks like zebra, but it is covered with black stripes. What have you been doing zebra? Why is it so hard to find you?"

39.

"Let us up," said the zebra, "and we'll show you." So they did. The zebra walked to some bushes where the sunlight fell all stripy. The giraffe walked to some trees where the shadows fell all blotchy.

"Now, where's your breakfast?"

40

So the man put his fingers close together and pressed them on the leopard's fur. Wherever they touched they left five little marks, close together. You can see them today on any leopard's skin you like.

45

"Now look at you!" said the man. "You can lie on the bare ground and look like a **heap of pebbles.**

46

You can lie on a branch and look like SUNShine through the leaves.

You can lie right across a path and look like nothing in particular. Those animals will never see you coming!"

47

So the leopard went away and lived **happily ever after.** That is all!

Purrrrr!

48

How the Rhinoceros got his Skin

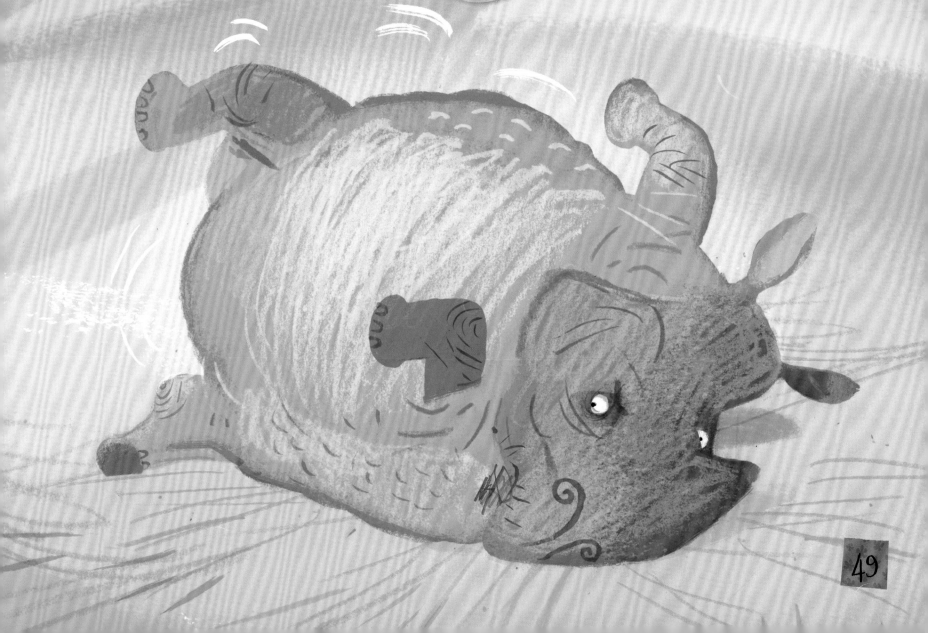

Once upon a time, on a lonely island
on the shores of the Red Sea,
there lived a man.

He owned nothing in the world
but his hat and his knife and a
cooking stove (of the kind that
you must particularly
never touch).

The man was very happy.
He had nothing to worry him.

Except...

...one rhinoceros, who lived in the very middle of the island.

He had a horn on his nose and two piggy eyes.

Hrumph!

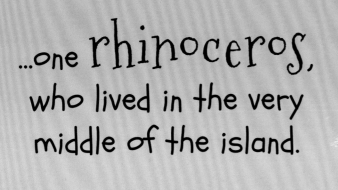

In those days the rhinoceros's skin fitted him quite tight. There were no wrinkles in it anywhere.

He had no manners then, and he has no manners now, and he never will have any manners.

One day the man took flour and water and currants and plums and sugar and other delicious things, and made himself one big cake.

It was two feet across and three feet thick.

He put it on the stove, and he baked it and he baked it till it was all beautifully brown.

It smelled YUMMY!

The rhinoceros smelled the delicious smell.
Just as the man was going to eat his cake,
along it came.

In two shakes of a tail,
the man climbed to the top
of a tall palm tree and hid.

57

The rhinoceros upset the stove with his nose, and the cake rolled onto the sand.

58

Then he spiked
that cake on the
horn of his nose,
and he ate it...

all up.

Every last crumb!

Then the rhinoceros went away
waving his tail, back to his home
in the very middle of the island.

60

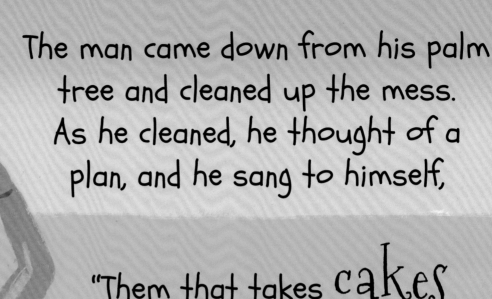

The man came down from his palm tree and cleaned up the mess. As he cleaned, he thought of a plan, and he sang to himself,

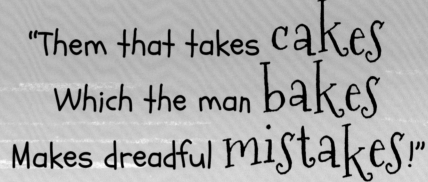

"Them that takes cakes
Which the man bakes
Makes dreadful mistakes!"

61

A few weeks later, there was a heat wave in the Red Sea. It was so hot that everybody took off their clothes. The man even took off his hat!

In those days the rhinoceros's skin buttoned underneath with three buttons.

The rhinoceros took
off his skin to have a
cooling swim
in the sea.

63

The rhinoceros did not say sorry to the man for eating his cake – he had no manners then, and he has no manners now...

and he never will have any manners.

splash!

He waddled straight into the water and blew bubbles through his nose, leaving his skin on the beach.

But the man found the skin, and he smiled a big smile. Then he danced three times round the skin and rubbed his hands.

The man filled his hat with crumbs. He had plenty, because he never ate anything but cake, and he never swept out his camp.

Then he took that skin, and he shook that skin, and he scrubbed that skin, and he rubbed that skin.

At last it was as full of
dry, stale, tickly
cake crumbs (and some
burned currants) as it
could possibly be.

Then the man climbed to the top
of his palm tree and waited.

When the rhinoceros came in from his swim, he put on his skin and buttoned it up with the three buttons.

And it tickled just like cake crumbs in bed.

Then he wanted to scratch, but that made it worse!

68

Then he lay down on the sands and
rolled and rolled...

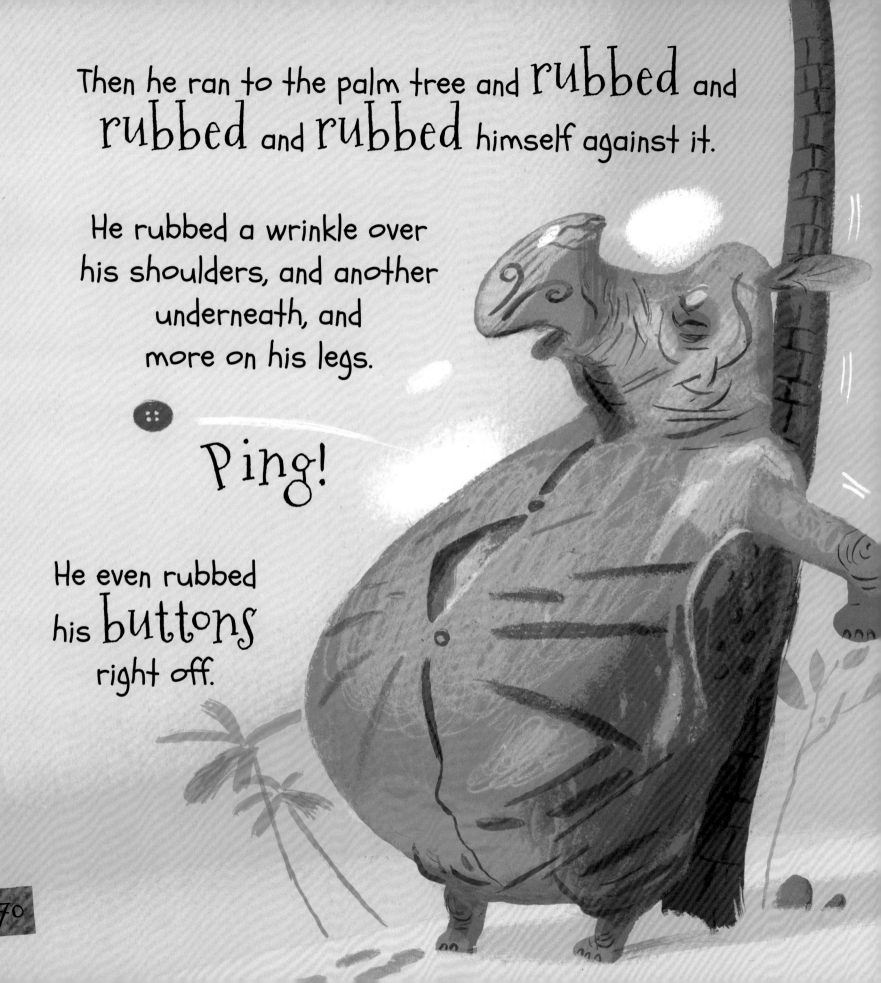

Then he ran to the palm tree and rubbed and rubbed and rubbed himself against it.

He rubbed a wrinkle over his shoulders, and another underneath, and more on his legs.

Ping!

He even rubbed his buttons right off.

It spoiled his temper, but it didn't make any difference to the crumbs. So he went home, very angry and horribly scratchy.

The man came down from his palm tree, and felt quite pleased with himself.

71

From that day to this, every rhinoceros has great folds in his skin and a **very bad temper**, all because of the cake crumbs inside.

Grrummph!

How the Whale got his Throat

Once upon a time
there was a whale, and he ate fish.

He ate the
starfish

and the
garfish

and the
crab

and the dab

74

and the
plaice

and the dace

and the really truly twirly-whirly eel.

He ate all the fish he
could find in all the sea. 75

One day the whale said,
"I'm hungry."

There was now only
one small fish left in all the
sea and he said, "Noble and
generous whale, have you
ever tasted man?"

"No," said the whale. "What is it like?"
"Nice," said the fish. "Nice but nubbly."

Splash!

"Then fetch me some," boomed the whale.

"One at a time is enough," said the clever fish. And he told the whale where he could find a man.

77

So the whale **swam** and **swam**
as fast as he could swim.

At **last**, in the middle of the sea,
he came to a **raft**.

On the raft was a **solitary**
shipwrecked sailor,
trailing his toes in the water.

78

He wore blue trousers held up with braces and he carried a knife, and they were the only things he had left in the world.

The whale opened his mouth
back, and **back,** and **back,**
till it nearly touched his tail,
and he swallowed the
sailor in his blue
trousers and braces,
and his raft, and
his knife.

Gulp!

80

He swallowed them all down into his
warm, dark, inside cupboards.
Then he smacked his lips, and turned round
three times on his tail.

But as soon as the sailor found himself inside the whale's warm, dark, inside cupboards...

and he **stumped**
and he **jumped**

he **thumped**
and he **bumped**

and he **hit**
and he **bit**

82

and he banged
and he clanged

and he hopped
and he dropped

and he
prowled
and he
howled

and he danced hornpipes
where he shouldn't.

The whale felt most unhappy indeed.
So he said to the clever little fish,

"This man is very nubbly,
and he is making me hiccup.
What shall I do?"

Hic!

"Tell him to come
out," said the fish.

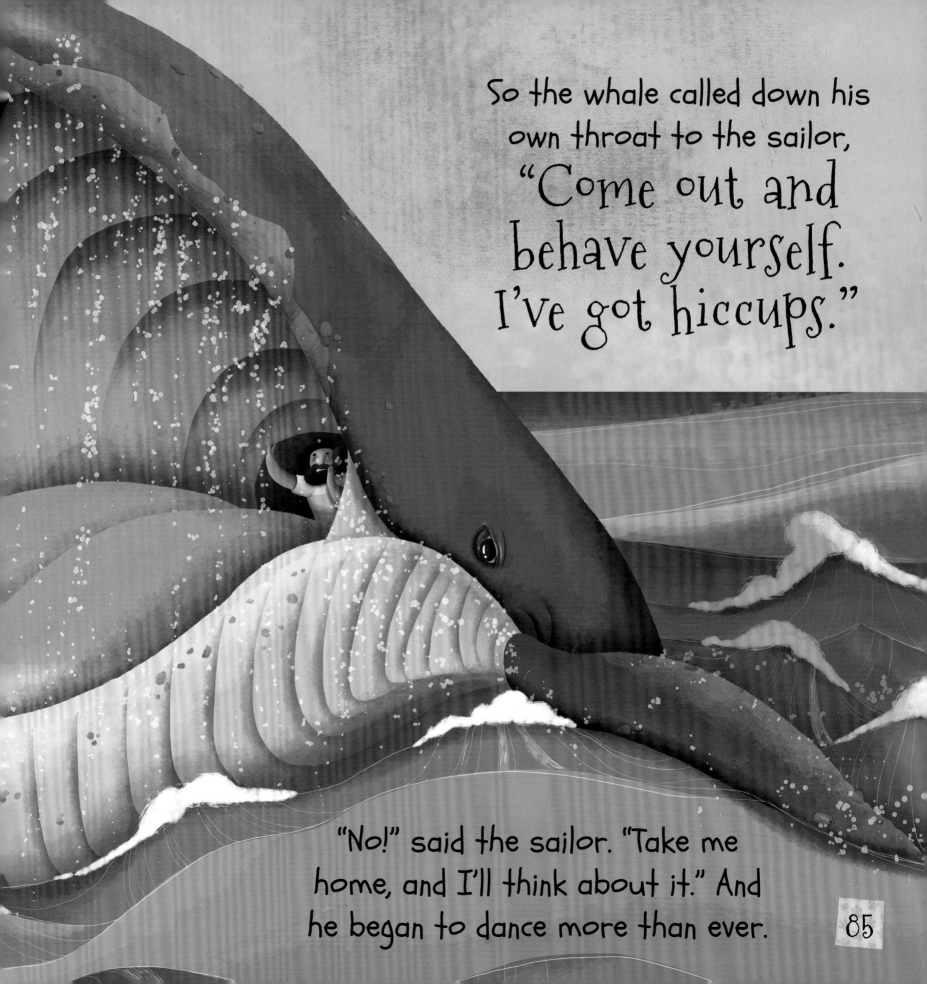

So the whale called down his
own throat to the sailor,
"Come out and
behave yourself.
I've got hiccups."

"No!" said the sailor. "Take me
home, and I'll think about it." And
he began to dance more than ever.

"You had better take him home," said the clever little fish.

So the whale SWAM and SWAM and SWAM, with both flippers and his tail – as hard as he could, with his hiccups.

Hiccup!

87

But while the whale was swimming, the sailor took his **knife** and cut up his **raft** to make a little square grating all running criss-cross.

He tied it firm with his **braces.**

88

And he wedged that grating good and tight into the whale's throat, and there it stuck!

89

At last the whale saw the shore and he rushed halfway up the beach, and opened his mouth wide and wide and wide, and said,

"We're at your stop!"

"Time to go!"

The sailor stepped out on the beach, and went home, where he married and lived happily ever after.

But before he went, he waved goodbye to the whale and sang,

"By means of a grating I've stopped your 'ating." 91

The clever little fish went and hid himself in the mud just under the door of the equator.

"Shhhhh!"

92

He was afraid that the whale might be angry with him.

And the whale didn't find him – not until he got out of his temper, and then they were good friends again.

93

From that day on, the grating in the whale's throat – which he could not cough up nor swallow down – stopped him eating anything except very, VERY small fish.

The starfish and the garfish and the crab and the dab and all the others were most relieved.

95

And that is the reason why whales today **never eat sailors** - or little boys or girls.